The Little Room

by **Chaim Desnick**

Illustrated by **Janet Zwebner**

PITSPOPANY

NEW YORK ◇ JERUSALEM

The Little Room
Published by Pitspopany Press
Text Copyright © 2004 by Chaim Desnick
Illustrations Copyright © 2004 by Janet Zwebner

Design: Benjie Herskowitz

Hard Cover ISBN: 1-930143-81-8
Soft Cover ISBN: 1-930143-86-9

Pitspopany Press titles may be purchased for fund raising programs
by schools and organizations by contacting:

Marketing Director, Pitspopany Press
40 East 78th Street, Suite 16D, New York, New York 10021
Tel: (800) 232-2931   Fax: (212) 472-6253
Email: pitspop@netvision.net.il
Website: www.pitspopany com

Printed in Israel

Once there was a little town and in that little town was a grocery store. It wasn't such a big grocery store, but it was big enough so that the people in the town could buy almost whatever they wanted. It was the only grocery store in the little town, so it was always very busy.

Fruit and Vegetables

In fact, it was so busy that every night after the store closed and David, the owner, went home, all the different sections of the store would argue about which of them had been the busiest during the day.

The Fruits and Vegetable Section would say, "I did the best! Just look at all the potatoes, tomatoes, cucumbers, and apples people bought today!"

The Meat and Chicken Section bragged, "You think that's good? Just look at all the meat and chicken I sold today. Why, there's barely a *pulka* left in my bin!"

The Canned Goods Section, the Drinks Section, the Baby Food Section, and the Cereals Section all chimed in, anxious to show off their half empty shelves.

The Cakes, Candies and Cookies Section was the worst. He always yelled the loudest, boasting about how many sweets he had sold, and all the little children who had eagerly gathered around his shelves to pick his goods.

"Why, I barely have any cookies left," he bragged, feeling very smug. "I would say my shelves are the most bare of all!" he added, for good measure.

Crackers

Cakes, Candies
and Cookies

Finest
Chocolates

Crackers

Rice
Cakes

Rice
Cakes

Choc Chip
Cookies

Gum
Balls

Licourice
Sticks

Wafers

Chocolate

Chocibar

All the Sections knew that having
empty shelves at the end of the day was a badge
of honor. The emptier the better. It meant that people
had bought your product.

Now, way in the back of the store, behind the Freezer Section and almost
to the Emergency Exit Door, was a little room that had empty shelves all the time.
You would think she was happy, but she wasn't.

When she heard all the Sections arguing about who had sold more of their goods, she was sad. After all, she had empty shelves, but no one ever came to fill them!

Once, the room had been very busy. The previous owner had used her shelves to store cooking oil, laundry detergent, and big bags of salt that were used during the winter to melt the ice on people's driveways.

But David had decided the Little Room was too far away from everything, and had moved all the bottles and bags into the main part of the store. Now, all that remained on the Little Room's shelves were some old newspapers, a colored-in coloring book, some rusty nails, a hammer, two puzzles with some pieces missing, and lots of dust.

Just after Purim, David began preparing for Passover.

"This year," he announced to his helpers, "I want us to have a big selection of Passover products.

"Why is that?" Tom, one of his helpers asked.

Meat and Chicken

PICKLES

CORN

PICKLES

CORN

PICKLES

CORN

"Because on Passover many Jews won't buy any bread or cookies, cereals or cakes, or anything made from grains or with yeast. They clean their houses to get rid of any trace of chametz, which is any food that is not kosher for Passover."

"Why is that?" Jack, another helper asked.

"Because it says so in the Torah, the Bible of the Jews," David explained. "And because yeast makes foods rise and look bigger than they really are, sort of like someone who brags. On Passover the Jews felt very humble, very thankful to God for taking them out of Egypt. They didn't feel boastful or proud. They certainly didn't feel bigger than they were."

The Kosher for Passover Guide

Tom and Jack nodded. Then they looked at all the shelves in all the sections.

"But we fill these shelves every day. Where are we going to put the Passover foods?" Tom wondered.

"I don't think we can stuff Passover foods in with the other foods," Jack pointed out.

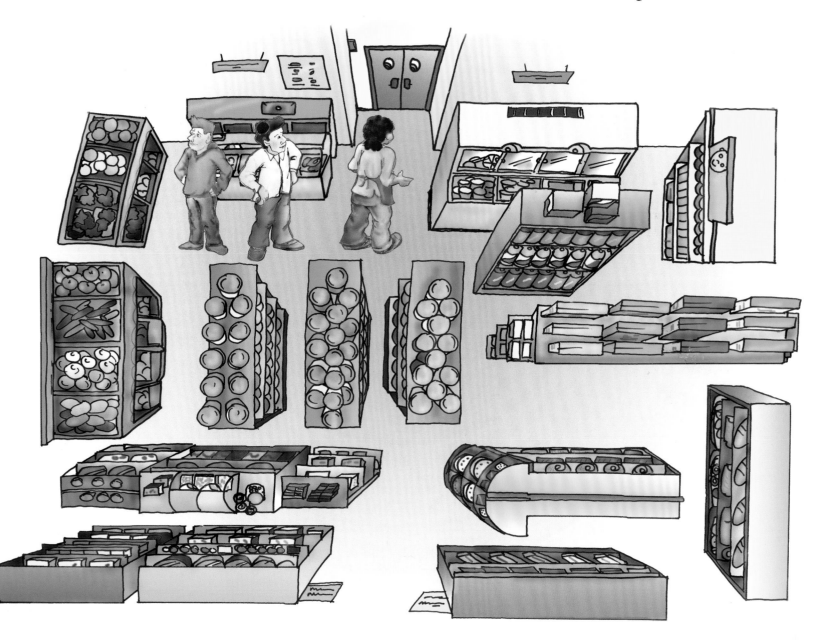

"No, of course not," David agreed. "Passover foods have to be on their own shelves in their own section. But where can we put them?"

"Why not use the Little Room in the back," suggested Tom. "It's pretty empty."

"Great idea," David said. "Let's prepare the room right away."

Jack and Tom went straight to work. First, they changed the burnt out fluorescent lights in the Little Room. Then, they took all the junk off the shelves and cleaned and washed the shelves until they sparkled.

The Little Room was very happy. It had been such a long time since she had had a bath.

Then, Jack put new shelf paper on the shelves while Tom swept the floor.

By now, the Little Room was so excited she fairly beamed. They were going to use her shelves again! They were going to bring in all sorts of wonderful foods for children and grownups to buy. She wouldn't have to be silent while all the other Sections talked about how everyone loved their goods. She would be able to brag about her section too.

But what was her Section?
No one had told her what her Section would be called.
And then, as quickly as Jack and Tom had come to clean her up, they left.

Weeks went by and the Little Room began to worry that everyone had forgotten about her again. Each night she would hear the other Sections bragging about how many people had bought their goods, but the Little Room was silent.

Then, one day a big truck pulled up behind the grocery store. Stack after stack of goods came out of the truck. There were boxes of matzo and cans of oil and jars of pickles and bottles of soda and packages of macaroons and just about everything a person could want – except chametz of course. There were so many different kinds of goods in the Little Room, but they had one thing in common. On each box, can, jar, bottle and package there were the words: **KOSHER FOR PASSOVER**

David supervised his helpers as
they started filling the shelves in the
Little Room. Soon there was hardly
any room on the shelves and they
started stacking boxes of goods
all along the walls of the Little Room.

"Well, that should do it," David said, looking around the room. "I think we bought enough for everyone for Passover." Then he put a big sign in front of the Little Room, PASSOVER SECTION, it read.

That week people came into the Little Room from early in the morning until late at night.

"Why David, I can't believe you've been hiding this room from us," one of the women, who usually bought from the other Sections, exclaimed. "It's such a lovely room and it's got everything we could want for Passover."

At night, the other Sections would mumble and complain.

"What's going on?" said the Canned Goods Section. "I see people walking around with canned goods, but they're not from my shelves."

"Well, how do you think I feel," cried the Cereals Section. "It's been three days now and my shelves are still almost full."

The Cakes and Cookies Section complained the most. "Is everyone on a diet?" he asked. "My breads have become positively stale!"

The Little Room wanted to brag about how her shelves were almost empty at the end of each day. But she realized that Passover was a special holiday where no one, not even a Little Room, should say anything that sounds like boasting or bragging. This was a time to just feel good and happy and satisfied.

But soon, too soon for the Little Room, Passover was over. Jack and Tom emptied the shelves in the Little Room. They took off the PASSOVER SECTION sign.

The Little Room was sad, especially when, once again, the other sections started bragging about how their shelves were emptying faster than David and his helpers could fill them.

But the Little Room was glad she hadn't bragged. She was a Passover Little Room, and bragging was...well, just not right.

All through the summer, fall, and winter the Little Room's shelves were bare. But she waited patiently. She knew that because of her, the people in the little town would have a happy Passover.

And that made her happy, too.

Also illustrated by Janet Zwebner